Thanks a Million

Poems by NIKKI GRIMES

Pictures by COZBI A. CABRERA

Greenwillow Books
An Imprint of HarperCollinsPublishers

Contents

Reward

"Thank you"
is a seed I plant
in the garden
of your heart.
Your smile
is the flower.
A slow and sweet surprise,
it blooms before my eyes!

Dear Teacher

If you tutor someone
twice a week
for 3 months,
when 2 months have 5 weeks,
and 1 month has 4,
what do you get?
Sparkling blackboards
9 Mondays in a row,
a straightened desk
no less than 16 times,
2 kisses (1 per cheek),
and 1 big, fat, THANKS!

Signed, David
who only hates math
1/2 as much
as he used to

The Lunchroom

My lunch tray's like a boulder
I've lugged around for miles,
past strangers, left and right,
whose unfamiliar smiles
are meant for someone else
'cause I'm the new kid here.
"You'll do fine," Mom said earlier.
"Of that I have no fear."

At least, I have a pie
that I don't have to share.
If no one will sit next to me,
why should I even care?
Oh, wait! Here comes a boy.
"I'm Max," he says. "Who're you?"
I smile and introduce myself—
then break my pie in two.

Lunch Box Love Notes

My baby brother's such a chore.
What do *I* have to watch him for?

"Please include him your play."
Mom asks so nice, what can I say?

If only she would understand,
I cannot *breathe* without his hand

tugging mine, while he squeals "Swing!"
I lift him high as anything

and spin him round until I drop.
That jumping bean just will not stop!

Why doesn't Mom appreciate
that what *I* want must always wait

until my brother's tucked in bed?
No more! I thought today, then read

the note Mom stuck in my lunch box.
"I love you right down to your socks.

For taking such good care of Ray,
I'll treat you to a film today."

Guess I'll keep helping Mom—for now,
and put up with that boy somehow.

Mystery

Rich or poor,
we all own
two tiny treasures.
Worthless if saved,
they are priceless when spent.
What are they?

("Thank you.")

Weekends

God invented weekends
and I'm thankful for that.
My weekends mean less homework.
Get out the ball and bat!

Just think: fun is official
at least two days a week.
So skateboard or play video games.
Go swim or scale a peak.

I might go to a movie
or choose to sleep all day.
Whatever I decide to do,
there's no work either way!

Weekends are worth having.
But I have one request:
Could You please lengthen them a bit?
I need six days of rest.

Shoe Surprise

He sails downcourt
and rattles the hoop
with slam dunks as mean as can be.
After jackhammering
the streets all week,
Dad finds time to coach me.

I used to think,
It's no big deal.
Don't all dads do that, too?
But I was wrong
as snow in June,
I learned from my friend Drew.

"You lucky, man,"
he said to me.
"I'd love to see the day
my father joined *me*
on the court.
He be's too busy to play."

His words sunk in
and scored this thought:
With my dad, I can't lose.
When he got home
that night, he found
I'd shined his boots and shoes.

Dear Author

When my father died last year,
Somebody threw a switch and turned me off.
I couldn't breathe. Or cry.
My family wondered why.

Months passed, and they figured
I must be okay. But they were wrong.
I leaked sadness everywhere I went.
No one seemed to notice or understand.
Until Lotus, the girl in your last book.
She was also drowning deep inside.
Some nights, I'd crawl between the pages
of that novel and hide for hours.

The two of you made all the difference.
I just thought you'd want to know.

Sincerely,
Grateful

The Good Neighbor

At dinnertime,
if Mom is late,
Miss Lee feeds me.
(Her cooking's great!)
I worry that
my whispered thanks
sound hollow as a ball.

One day last fall,
to even the score,
I left a Snickers
by her front door
then rang the bell
and ran before she came.

I know she loved
her dark surprise.
I catch the sparklers
in her eyes
when she tells me
about her "secret sweetie."

Scout's Honor

I tripped,
humiliated by
a loose lace.
Laughter scarred
every single face
but yours.
Scout's honor,
I'll carry your backpack
forever.

Even the Trees

Trees, arms raised in praise,
demonstrate the attitude
of gratitude. Look!

Shelter

I wish these walls were ours.
I wish this bed were mine,
that dinnertime meant just us three,
my brother, mom, and me.

I wish I had a room
that I was forced to clean.
I'd gripe to my best friend, then say,
"Come to my house and play."

Things could be worse, I know.
At least, I'm not alone.
My mom and brother hold me tight
when I cry late at night.

A Lesson from the Deaf

First, sweep one hand
up to your mouth,
as if to blow a velvet kiss.
Like this.

Second, drop that hand
into the other,
crisscross, open palms staring
at the sky.
Do you see?
How your clever hands
create a butterfly?

(Think of shadows
you shape upon a wall at night.
But this is more than play.)

Stand before someone
who has been kind to you.
Follow steps one and two,
and without breathing a word,
your "thank you" will be heard.

Unspoken

Mom's birthday comes
the same time every year.

As always
you forgot.

Did too! Unless it was
someone else who asked
to sign my card.

I've done it a gazillion times.

That's what you always say.

By the way, tonight
when Mom told me

Why'd you jump up, instead?

Mom looked at you as if
your skin turned green.

Mom's birthday comes
the same time every year.

Did not!

Look, it's tough
to find the perfect one
You've done it "a gazillion times."
I know. But wait till next year.

"Jen, it's your turn
to do the dishes."

Maybe I lost my head.

Mom looked at me as if
my hair turned green.

"You *hate* doing dishes," she said.

Still, you washed them, didn't you?

Why?

Oh, yes it was.
Is it because you wanted to say—

Well, anyway. You're welcome.

It's true.

Yeah.
Why?
Because. . . . It wasn't a big deal.

Forget it! Just forget it!

A Round of Thanks

The turkey lies waiting
while we bow for grace
to offer up thanks
for this time and place:

For a spot on the swim team.
For a chance to run track.
For Gram, who lived far away
and has finally moved back.

For this creaky old house
with the patched-up roof.
For my sister, the pest.
For my brother, the goof.

For this table of tongue-teasing
treasures heaped high.
For stuffing, roast turkey,
and hot apple pie.

We give thanks, Lord.
We give thanks.

For my agent, Elizabeth Harding,
to whom I can never say
thank you often enough
—N.G.

For Chloe, Isaiah, Asia, Gabriel,
Jonathan, Imani, and Kimathi,
as they blaze their way
—C.A.C.

Thanks a Million
Text copyright © 2006 by Nikki Grimes
Illustrations copyright © 2006 by Cozbi A. Cabrera
All rights reserved. Printed in the United States of America.

For information address HarperCollins Children's Books,
a division of HarperCollins Publishers,
195 Broadway, New York, NY 10007.
www.harpercollinschildrens.com

Acrylic paints were used for the full-color art.
The text type is Mrs. Eaves.

Library of Congress Cataloging-in-Publication Data
Grimes, Nikki.
Thanks a million / by Nikki Grimes;
pictures by Cozbi A. Cabrera.
p. cm.
"Greenwillow Books."

ISBN 978-0-06-320403-4 (pbk.)

1. Children's poetry, American. I. Cabrera, Cozbi A., ill. II. Title.
PS3557.R489982T47 2005 813'.54—dc22 2004054158

24 25 PC 10 9 8 7 6 5

First Greenwillow paperback, 2021

Greenwillow Books